Babushka

To the Children of Southampton
Friends' Meeting – S. A. H.

To Francesco, all my love for
a peaceful life – S. F.

Barefoot Books
3 Bow Street, 3rd Floor
Cambridge, MA 02138

Text copyright © 2002 by Sandra Ann Horn. Illustrations copyright © 2002 by Sophie Fatus
The moral right of Sandra Ann Horn to be identified as the author and Sophie Fatus
to be identified as the illustrator of this work has been asserted

First published in The United States of America in 2002 by Barefoot Books, Inc.

This book is printed on 100% acid-free paper. This book was typeset in Abbess 20 on 28 point. The illustrations were prepared in acrylics.
Graphic design by Judy Linard, London. Color separation by Grafiscan, Verona, Italy. Printed and bound in China

3 5 7 9 8 6 4

Library of Congress Cataloging-in-Publication Data

Horn, Sandra Ann.
   Babushka / retold by Sandra Ann Horn ; illustrated by Sophie Fatus.
      p. cm.
   Summary: While traveling, Babushka gives her gifts for the Christ child
   away and thinks she has nothing left to give the baby, only to discover
   that everything she gave away, she also gave to him.
   ISBN 1-84148-353-2
   1. Folklore–Russia. 2. Christmas–Folklore.   I. Fatus, Sophie, ill.
II. Title.
   PZ8.1.H859 Bae 2002
   398.2'0947'02--dc21

                              00-010728

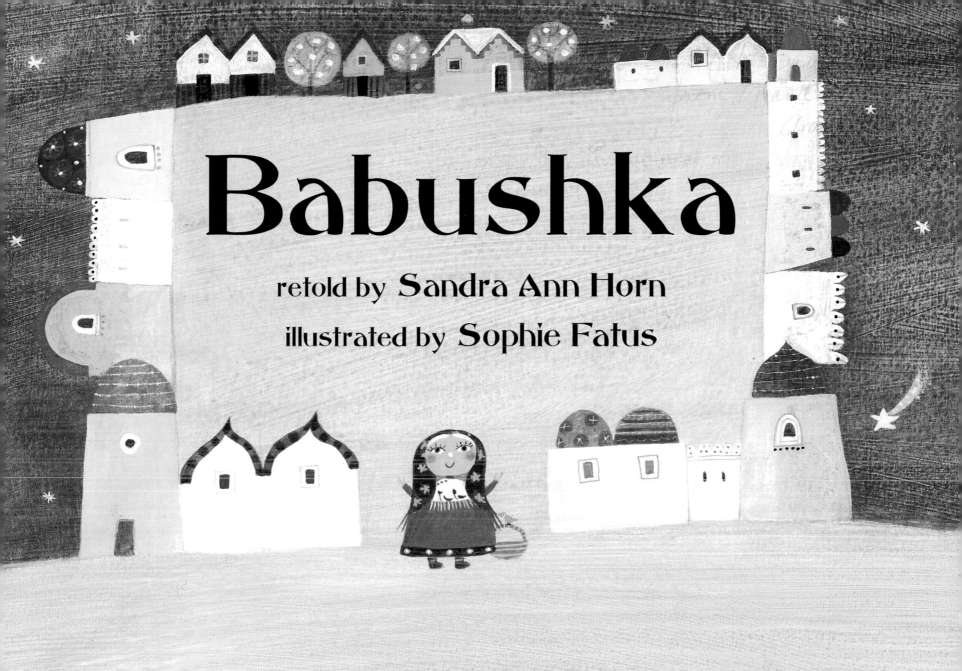

Babushka

retold by Sandra Ann Horn

illustrated by Sophie Fatus

Barefoot Books
Celebrating Art and Story

Long ago, far away, there lived
a little old woman. She was as
round and kindly as a warm
plum pudding, but she didn't stop
sweeping, dusting and polishing
from sunrise to starshine.

There was not a speck of dust or a spider's web in her house. She kept busy all the time because there was an empty place in her heart and it made her sad to think about it.

One evening Babushka was polishing her candlesticks when a bright new star shone in through the window.

"Why, there's a mark on the windowpane," said Babushka. "I haven't noticed that before. What a disgrace."
The star hid behind a cloud.

Babushka began to rub the windowpane. She looked out and saw an angel in the garden. "Good news!" sang the angel.

"You'll have to wipe your feet if you want to come in," said Babushka.

The angel flew away.

There was a knock at the door. There stood
three kings with golden crowns.

"Come in, your majesties," said Babushka,
"but please take off your royal boots."

"We have followed the star," they said, "to
find the new baby king. Would you like to
come with us?"

"I haven't got time to go journeying about!"
she said. "What about the washing up?"

The kings' camels were standing by the gate.
"Oh!" said Babushka. "Muddy feet on my clean path! Shoo! Shoo!!" and she flapped her dust cloth.

The camels took fright and galloped away, and the kings went chasing after them.

"I'll just rest my feet for a little," said Babushka, "before I dust the canary."

No sooner had she sat down than her head began to nod, and she fell asleep.

The angel came back, and sang about a baby born in a stable, with nothing but a swaddling cloth to wrap him in.

The star peeped out from behind the cloud and shone in through the window, full on Babushka's sleeping face. She woke up.

"Bless me!" she said. "A baby in a scruffy stable full of cattle? And not even a warm shawl to wrap him in! I must set off at once."

She packed a basket with a little toy clown, a warm shawl and a bottle of ginger cordial for the grownups, and set off. The sky was lit up as bright as day by the star, and crowded with angels, but Babushka did not look up.

"All this dust on the road! It's a scandal!" she said.

Babushka had not gone far when she saw a woman and a little girl by the side of the road. The girl was crying.

"What's the matter, dearie?" said Babushka.

"We were running to see the new king, and she dropped her dolly," said the girl's mother.

"I put her in my pocket, and she must have fallen out," the little girl sobbed.

Babushka took the toy clown out of her basket and jiggled him to make him dance. The child stopped crying and laughed.

"Take it, with my love," said Babushka.

Babushka had not gone much farther when she met a little old woman, hobbling along and moaning.

"What's the matter, my dear?" asked Babushka.

"I want to see the new baby," said the little old woman, "but I can't get along very fast because my legs ache so much."

"Here," said Babushka, "take this cordial with my love. It'll do you a power of good."

The old woman took a big drink and trotted away with a smile on her face and a blessing on her lips.

Around the corner Babushka came
upon a shepherd boy, carrying a
newborn lamb. He was shivering.
   "I couldn't keep up with the others,"
he said. "My arms are so cold that I
can't carry this lamb much farther.
It's a present for the new baby king."
   Babushka wrapped the shawl snugly
around his shoulders.
   "Take this, with my love," she said. "It
will keep you warm on your journey."

Babushka went on her way. The basket felt as light as air. She stopped and looked inside. It was empty!

"You silly old woman," she said to herself. "You've given all the presents away."

Sadly, she turned back the way she had come. "I can't greet the baby without a gift," she said.

Just then she heard a voice calling,
"Babushka!"
It was Mary.
Babushka hung back. "I have no gift,"
she said.
"Please come in," Mary smiled.

Babushka went in, and there was the baby wrapped in the warm shawl. The little clown was beside him in the manger. Joseph was pouring a glass of cordial.

"But I gave all the gifts away!" said Babushka.

"Everything you gave with love, you gave to my son, also," said Mary.

Babushka gazed around her. "Look at the cobwebs," she said. "I'll just tidy up."

Then the baby held out his arms and smiled. His eyes were like the deep, starry night. In his smile was love itself.

A strange feeling crept over Babushka. She forgot about tidying up.

"Would you like to hold him?" asked Mary.

Babushka took the baby in her arms.

All the animals crowded around. Babushka stroked the old gray donkey's nose. He nuzzled her ear. The baby chuckled and so did Babushka. She held him close.

"Peace," sang the angels.